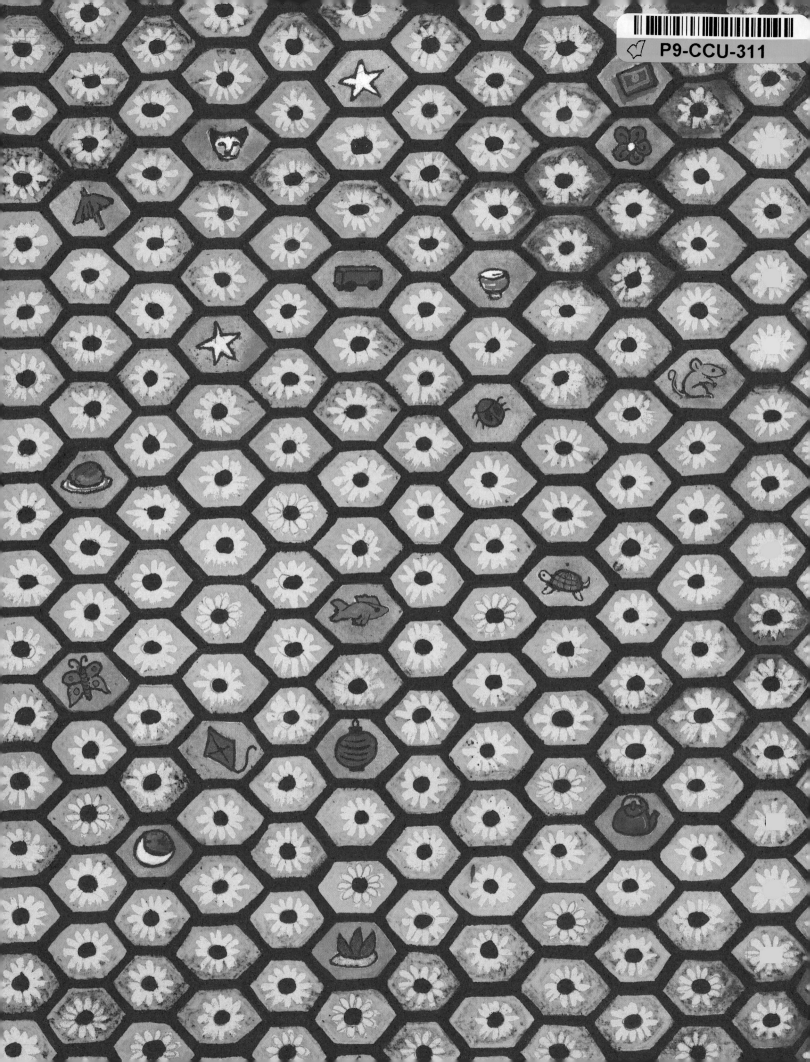

# CHINESE
## AND ENGLISH
## NURSERY RHYMES

### SHARE AND SING IN TWO LANGUAGES

Faye-Lynn Wu

*Illustrations by*
**Kieren Dutcher**

**TUTTLE** Publishing

Tokyo | Rutland, Vermont | Singapore

Published by Tuttle Publishing, an imprint of Periplus Editions (HK) Ltd.

**www.tuttlepublishing.com**

**Library of Congress Cataloging-in-Publication Data**

Wu, Faye-Lynn.
 Chinese and English nursery rhymes : share and sing in two languages / Faye-Lynn Wu ; illustrations by Kieren Dutcher. -- 1st ed.
     p. cm.
 Summary: A collection of nursery rhymes in English and Chinese, some originating from each tradition, interspersed with facts about Chinese culture and traditions.
 ISBN 978-0-8048-4094-1 (hardcover)
1.  Nursery rhymes, Chinese. 2.  Children's poetry, Chinese. [1. Nursery rhymes. 2. Poetry. 3. Chinese language materials--Bilingual.]  I. Dutcher, Kieren, ill. II. Title.
 PL2309.C45C47 2010
 398.80951--dc22
                          2009031567

ISBN 978-0-8048-4094-1

**Distributed by**

**North America, Latin America & Europe**
Tuttle Publishing
364 Innovation Drive
North Clarendon, VT 05759-9436 U.S.A.
Tel: 1 (802) 773-8930
Fax: 1 (802) 773-6993
info@tuttlepublishing.com
www.tuttlepublishing.com

**Asia Pacific**
Berkeley Books Pte. Ltd.
61 Tai Seng Avenue #02-12
Singapore 534167
Tel: (65) 6280-1330
Fax: (65) 6280-6290
inquiries@periplus.com.sg
www.periplus.com

First edition
12  11  10            5  4  3  2

Printed in Singapore

To my husband, Alex, and children, Benjamin and Rachel,
for their love, patience, and support.
—FW


To Dan, Sophie and William.
I couldn't have done it without you!
—KD

Our sincere thanks to our family, friends, and colleagues in the CD song production—Madeleine King, a fantastic musician, for her creative songwriting and lovely music; the singers, PJ (Paul) Robinson, Caroline Portante, Adella K. Cho, Cathy (Lan Qi) Li, Shihua Liu, and Hui Qiao Wu; Menna Stern for her technical support; and John Carlstroem and Siu-mui Woo for their support behind the scenes.

# Introduction

When my son was born, I read him Mother Goose rhymes and sang my favorite childhood songs in Chinese to ease my own homesickness. Not only did I have fun learning the English rhymes with my son, but I also passed my Chinese heritage down to him through singing and acting out my old favorites. I can still see his sleepy face and hear his childish voice begging for more rhymes: "Sing, mommy, sing."

Children naturally love music and verse, so it is no wonder that nursery rhymes appeal to us as children and stay with us throughout our lives. What could be a more enjoyable way to learn a different culture and language than through rhymes and songs?

Bugs, trains, counting: we've paired the rhymes by shared themes, so for each, there's a Chinese rhyme and an English rhyme to delight in. We invite young readers and adults to explore the magic of children's rhymes and the universal quality of the shared world of childhood. We also provide notes throughout the book so that you can learn more about Chinese culture.

Whether you are a native Chinese speaker or English speaker, you can learn the rhymes and songs—simply follow the words as you sing, or join in the chorus on the audio CD.

## Enjoy!

*Faye-Lynn Wu and Kieren Dutcher*

# Contents

# Rig-a-Jig-Jig

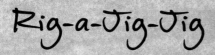

As I was walking down the street,
Down the street,
Down the street,
A pretty girl (boy) I chanced to meet
Heigh–ho, heigh–ho, heigh–ho.

Rig–a–jig–jig and away we go, away we go
Away we go
Rig–a–jig–jig and away we go
Heigh–ho, heigh–ho, heigh–ho.

# When We Are Together
## 当我们同在一起
**dāng wǒ men tóng zài yì qǐ**

当我们同在一起
**dāng wǒ men tóng zài yì qǐ**
When we are together

在一起, 在一起
**zài yì qǐ, zài yì qǐ**
Together, together

当我们同在一起
**dāng wǒ men tóng zài yì qǐ**
When we are together

其快乐无比
**qí kuài lè wú bǐ**
We are so happy

你对着我笑嘻嘻
**nǐ duì zhē wǒ xiào xī xī**
Smiling, you look at me

我对着你笑哈哈
**wǒ duì zhe nǐ xiào hā hā**
Laughing, I look back at you

当我们同在一起
**dāng wǒ men tóng zài yì qǐ**
When we are together

其快乐无比
**qí kuài lè wú bǐ**
We are so happy.

# Kites Go Up

The kites go up,
the kites go down,
In and around,
all over the town.

The children run
and jump and play,
Because they love
a windy day.

# Jumping Rope
跳绳
**tiào shéng**

绳子抡的团团转
**shéng zi lun de túan túan zhuàn**
The jump rope turns round and round.

妹妹进来跳跳看
**mèi mei jìn lái tiào tiào kàn**
Little sister, please come and try
jumping in

一二三四五六七
**yī èr sān sì wǔ liù qī**
One two three four five six seven

跳得过的尽你玩
**tiào de guò dē jìn nǐ wán**
Play as long as you can jump

一二三四五六七
**yī èr sān sì wǔ liù qī**
One two three four five six seven

跳不过的就要换
**tiào bú guò dē jiù yào huàn**
If you can't, then wait your turn.

## Do you know ...

Kites were invented in China about 2,000 years ago. They were originally designed to use in wars to spy on enemies or send messages. Later, kites were used for fun.

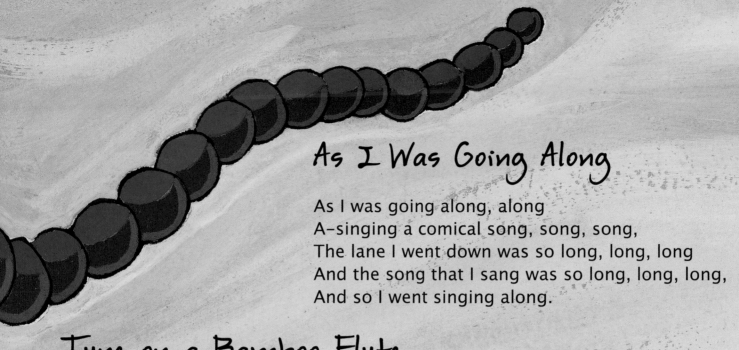

## As I Was Going Along

As I was going along, along
A-singing a comical song, song, song,
The lane I went down was so long, long, long
And the song that I sang was so long, long, long,
And so I went singing along.

## Tune on a Bamboo Flute

紫竹调
**zǐ zhú diào**

一根紫竹直苗苗
**yì gēn zǐ zhú zhí miáo miáo**
One straight bamboo stick

送给宝宝做管箫
**sòng gěi bǎo bǎo zùo guǎn xiāo**
Makes a pipe for the baby

箫儿对正口
**xiāor duì zhèng kǒu**
Lining up the flute with the mouth

口儿对正箫
**kǒur duì zhèng xiāo**
Putting the mouth on the flute

箫中吹出时新调
**xiāo zhōng chuī chū shí xīn diào**
The flute creates new tunes

小宝宝一滴一滴学会了
**xiāo bǎo bǎo yì dī yì dī xué huì liǎo**
Step by step little baby learns to play

小宝宝一滴一滴学会了
**xiāo bǎo bǎo yì dī yì dī xué huì liǎo**
Step by step little baby learns to play.

# Ladybug

Ladybug, ladybug
Fly away home
Your house is on fire
Your children all gone.

All but one,
and her name is Ann
She crept under
the frying pan.

# Little Bugs
## 小虫虫
### xiǎo chóng chóng

虫虫虫虫飞
**chóng chóng chóng chóng fēi**
Bugs fly

两只虫虫斗斗嘴
**liǎng zhī chóng chóng dòu dòu zuǐ**
Two bugs fight

大虫跟着走
**dà chóng gēn zhe zǒu**
The big bug follows

小虫要娘背
**xiǎo chóng yào niáng bēi**
The baby bug wants to be carried.

# I Am a Little Bird
## 我是只小小鸟
## wǒ shì zhī xiǎo xiǎo niǎo

我是只小小鸟
I am a little bird
**wǒ shì zhī xiǎo xiǎo niǎo**

飞就飞，叫就叫
**fēi jiù fēi, jiào jiù jiào**
Soaring and chirping

自由逍遥
**zì yóu xiāo yáo**
Freely and happily

我不知有烦恼
**wǒ bù zhī yǒu fán nǎo**
I have no worries

我不知有忧愁
**wǒ bù zhī yǒu yōu chóu**
I have no sadness

只是爱欢笑
**zhǐ shì ài huān xiào**
I only love to laugh.

## Birds

Once I saw a little bird
Come hop, hop, hop
And I cried, "Little bird,
Will you stop, stop, stop?"
I was going to the window
To say, How do you do?
But then he shook his little tail
And away he flew.

### Do you know ...

The Chinese admire nature. These are the plants that represent each of the four seasons:

* Spring...orchid 春兰 **chūn lán**
* Summer...lotus 夏荷 **xià hé**
* Autumn...chrysanthemum 秋菊 **qiū jú**
* Winter...plum blossom 冬梅 **dōng méi**

Can you find these flowers in the garden?

# One Two Three Four Five

One two three four five,
Once I caught a fish alive
Six seven eight nine ten,
Then I let it go again.

Why did you let it go?
Because it bit my finger so.
Which finger did it bite?
The little finger on the right.

12

# One Two Three, Climb Up the Mountain

## 一二三，爬上山
## yī èr sān pá shàng shān

一二三，爬上山
**yī èr sān pá shàng shān**
One two three, climb up the mountain

四五六，翻跟头
**sì wǔ liù fān gēn tóu**
Four five six, somersault

七八九，拍皮球
**qī bā jiǔ pāi pí qiú**
Seven eight nine, bounce the ball

伸出两只手
**shēn chū liǎng zhī shǒu**
Put out two hands

十个手指头
**shí ge shǒu zhǐ tóu**
Ten fingers in all.

### Do you know ...

Everywhere in the world, people use their hands to communicate with each other. This is how Chinese children count on their hands from 1 to 10.

Can you do it? Is it different from the way you count on your hands?

13

# I Hear Thunder

I hear thunder
I hear thunder
Hark, don't you?
Hark, don't you?

Pitter-patter rain drops
Pitter-patter rain drops
I'm wet through
So are you.

# The Rain Is Coming
## 下雨歌
## xià yǔ gē

淅沥淅沥哗啦哗啦
**xīlī xīlī huālā huālā**
Sili-sili wha-la wha-la

雨下来了
**yǔ xià lái le**
The rain is coming down

我的妈妈来了，来了
**wǒ de māma lái le lái le**
My mom is coming, coming

拿着一把伞
**ná zhe yì bǎ sǎn**
Holding an umbrella

淅沥淅沥哗啦哗啦
**xīlī xīlī huālā huālā**
Sili-sili wha-la wha-la

啦啦啦
**lā lā lā**
La la la.

# I Love Little Pussy

I love little Pussy
Her coat is so warm
And if I don't hurt her
She'll do me no harm.

So I'll not pull her tail
Nor drive her away
But Pussy and I
Very gently will play.

# Little Kitten

小猫咪
**xiǎo māo mī**

小猫咪
**xiǎo māo mī**
Little kitten

过河西
**guò hé xī**
Crossing the West River

跟奶奶
**gēn nǎi nǎi**
Following grandma

吃东西
**chī dōng xī**
To find some food

扯花布
**chě huā bù**
Playing with beautiful fabric

做花衣
**zuò huā yī**
To make fancy clothing.

# Hickory Dickory Dock

Hickory dickory dock
The mouse went up the clock.

The clock struck one
The mouse ran down

Hickory dickory dock.
Hickory dickory dock.

# Little Mouse
# 小老鼠
## xiǎo lǎo shǔ

小老鼠上灯台
**xiǎo lǎo shǔ shàng dēng tái**
The little mouse climbed up the lamp

偷油吃
**tōu yóu chī**
To find some oil to nibble

下不来
**xià bù lái**
Can't get down

喵喵喵
**miāo miāo miāo**
Meow, meow, meow

猫来了
**māo lái le**
Here came the cat

叽哩咕噜滚下来
**jī lī gū lū gǔn xià lái**
Ji-li-gu-lu down fell the mouse.

## Do you know ...

Chinese people use paper to make colorful lanterns. Long ago, people hung lanterns to chase away evil spirits. Today people hang lanterns for good luck and decoration. At celebrations for New Year, other holidays, and weddings, you see beautiful lanterns on the streets, in parks, and at temples.

The little mice are too scared to come down. Can you help the little mice find their mother?

17

# To Market, to Market

To market, to market, to buy a fat pig;
Home again, home again, jiggetty–jig.

To market, to market, to buy a fat hog;
Home again, home again, jiggetty–jog.

To market, to market, to buy a plum bun;
Home again, home again, market is done.

## Tricycle

三轮车
**sān lún chē**

三轮车
**sān lún chē**
Tricycle

跑得快
**pǎo de kuài**
Pedaling so fast

上面坐个老太太
**shàng miàn zuò ge lǎo tài tài**
Ridden by an old lady

要五毛给一块
**yào wǔ máo gěi yí kuài**
I asked for five cents,
she gave me one dollar

你说奇怪不奇怪
**nǐ shuō qí guài bù qí guài**
How strange is that!

## Muffin Man

Oh, do you know the muffin man,
The muffin man, the muffin man,
Oh, do you know the muffin man,
That lives on Drury Lane?

Oh, yes, I know the muffin man,
The muffin man, the muffin man.
Oh, yes, I know the muffin man
That lives on Drury Lane.

## Doughnuts for Sale

卖油条
**mài yóu tiáo**

街头巷尾卖油条
**jiē tóu xiàng wěi mài yóu tiáo**
Doughnuts for sale along the streets

卖来卖去卖不掉
**mài lái mài qù mài bú diào**
All day he couldn't sell them

哗啦啦啦啦啦变成老油条
**huā lā lā lā lā lā biàn chéng lǎo yóu tiáo**
Hua-la-la-la-la-la they all got stale.

## Do you know ...

Have you been to a farmers' market where there are people selling fresh fruit and vegetables, meat, fish, and tasty treats? Traditionally, Chinese people go to the market every day to shop for fresh food. Going to the market is fun: you meet neighbors and friends.

Imagine you are planning for your birthday party. Can you find all the things you need at this market?

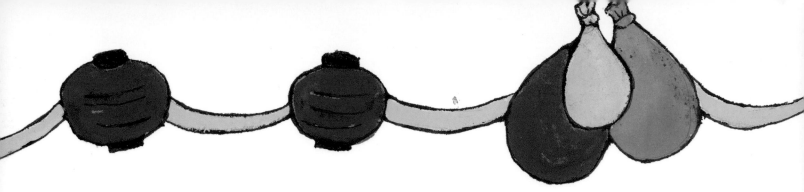

# Happy Birthday to You

Happy birthday to you
Happy birthday to you
Happy birthday dear ...
Happy birthday to you.

### Do you know ...

It is common that Chinese don't celebrate their children's birthdays every year, but they honor children's one-month-old and one-year-old birthdays. After the first birthday, the next important birthday celebration is at 60 years old.

Noodles and peaches are symbols of long life, so long noodles and peach-shaped steamed buns are served at birthday parties.

Look at the presents brought for the baby's one-month birthday. Can you find the presents for the baby—a pair of gold bracelets from the grandma, four red eggs from the neighbor, a silver necklace from the auntie, and lucky money in a red envelope from the uncle?

20

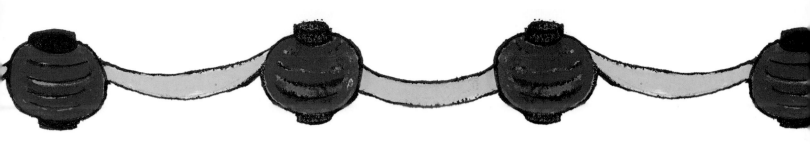

# Happy Birthday to You

祝你生日快乐

**zhù nǐ shēng rì kuài lè**

祝你生日快乐
**zhù nǐ shēng rì kuài lè**
Happy birthday to you

祝你生日快乐
**zhù nǐ shēng rì kuài lè**
Happy birthday to you

祝你生日快乐
**zhù nǐ shēng rì kuài lè**
Happy birthday to you

祝你生日快乐
**zhù nǐ shēng rì kuài lè**
Happy birthday to you.

# I'm a Little Teapot

I'm a little teapot
Short and stout
Here is my handle
Here is my spout.

When I get all steamed up
Then I shout
Tip me over and pour me out!

# Little Sister

妹妹背着洋娃娃
**mèi mei bēi zhe yáng wā wā**

妹妹背着洋娃娃
**mèi mei bēi zhe yáng wā wā**
Little sister carries her baby doll

走到花园来看花
**zǒu dào huā yuán lái kàn huā**
Walks to the garden to see the flowers

娃娃哭了叫妈妈
**wā wā kū le jiào māma**
The baby doll cries for its mother

树上小鸟笑哈哈
**shù shàng xiǎo niǎo xiào hā hā**
The bird laughs from the treetops.

# Three Young Rats with Black Felt Hats

Three young rats with black felt hats,
Three young ducks with white straw flats,
Three young dogs with curling tails,
Three young cats with demi-veils.

Went out to walk with two young pigs
In satin vests and sorrel wigs,
But suddenly it chanced to rain,
And so they all went home again.

### Do you know ...

More than 2,000 years ago,
Chinese invented the zodiac
animals to keep track of years.
Each year is matched to one of the
12 animals at the top of the page.
Many Chinese still use the zodiac
animals to tell someone their age.

Can you find all of the zodiac
animals in the picture?

horse
马 **mǎ**

sheep/goat 羊 **yáng**

猴 **hóu** monkey

rooster
鸡 **jī**

dog 狗 **gǒu**

pig
猪 **zhū**

# Two Tigers

## 两只老虎
## liǎng zhī lǎo hǔ

两只老虎, 两只老虎
**liǎng zhī lǎo hǔ , liǎng zhī lǎo hǔ**
Two tigers, two tigers

跑得快, 跑得快
**pǎo de kuài, pǎo de kuài**
Run very fast, run very fast

一只没有耳朵
**yì zhī méi yǒu ěr duō**
One without an ear

一只没有尾巴
**yì zhī méi yǒu wěi bā**
One without a tail

真奇怪, 真奇怪
**zhēn qí guài, zhēn qí guài**
How strange, how strange.

## The Train
火车快飞
**huǒ chē kuài fēi**

火车快飞
**huǒ chē kuài fēi**
The train speeding fast

火车快飞
**huǒ chē kuài fē**
The train speeding fast

穿过高山
**chuān guò gāo shān**
Going through the mountains

渡过小溪
**dù guò xiǎo xī**
Crossing the rivers

不知穿过几百里
**bù zhī chuān guò jǐ bǎi lǐ**
How many li it travels!

搭到家里搭到家
**dā dào jiā lǐ dā dào jiā lǐ**
Taking me home, taking me home

妈妈看见真欢喜
**māma kàn jiàn zhēn huān xǐ**
Mama is so happy to see me.

# Down by the Station

Down by the station
Early in the morning
See the little puffer–bellies all in a row.

See the engine driver
Pull the little handle
Chug, chug, poof, poof,
Off we go!

# The Moon Is Rising
# 月亮出来了
**yuè liàng chū lái liǎo**

月亮出来了
**yuè liàng chū lái liǎo**
The moon is rising

月亮出来了
**yùe lìang chū lái liǎo**
The moon is rising

弯弯黄黄挂在椰树梢
**wān wān huáng huáng guà zài yé shù shāo**
Its crescent yellow shape dangling in the coconut tree

羊儿看见了喜的咩咩叫
**yáng er kàn jiàn liǎo xǐ de miē miē jiào**
The sheep look at the moon bleating with delight

它喊宝宝快来瞧
**tā hǎn bǎo bao kuài lái qiáo**
And call their babies to see

椰子树上结香蕉
**yé zi shù shàng jié xiāng jiāo**
The banana-growing coconut tree.

# I See the Moon
I see the moon
And the moon sees me
The moon sees the somebody I'd like to see.
God bless the moon
And God bless me
God bless the somebody I'd like to see!

## Little Stars
## 小星星
**xiǎo xīng xīng**

一闪一闪亮晶晶
**yì shǎn yì shǎn liàng jīng jīng**
Twinkling, twinkling, shining bright

满天都是小星星
**mǎn tiān dōu shì xiǎo xīng xīng**
The sky is full of little stars

高挂天上放光明
**gāo guà tiān shàng fàng guāng míng**
High up in the sky so bright

好象许多小眼睛
**hǎo xiàng xǔ duō xiǎo yǎn jīng**
Like many tiny shining eyes.

一闪一闪亮晶晶
**yì shǎn yì shǎn liàng jīng jīng**
Twinkling, twinkling, shining bright

满天都是小星星
**mǎn tiān dōu shì xiǎo xīng xīng**
The sky is full of little stars.

## Twinkle, Twinkle, Little Star

Twinkle, twinkle, little star
How I wonder what you are
Up above the world so high
Like a diamond in the sky
Twinkle, twinkle little star
How I wonder what you are.

### Do you know ...

Chinese people follow the lunar calendar. You can watch this calendar change by looking at the shape of the moon. For example, the full moon means that it is the 15th of the Chinese lunar month.

It's fun to see the moon change its shape over a course of days! Find a time at night to go outside and look at the moon. Draw a picture of it. Do this for at least a week. Compare your drawings.

What do you see?

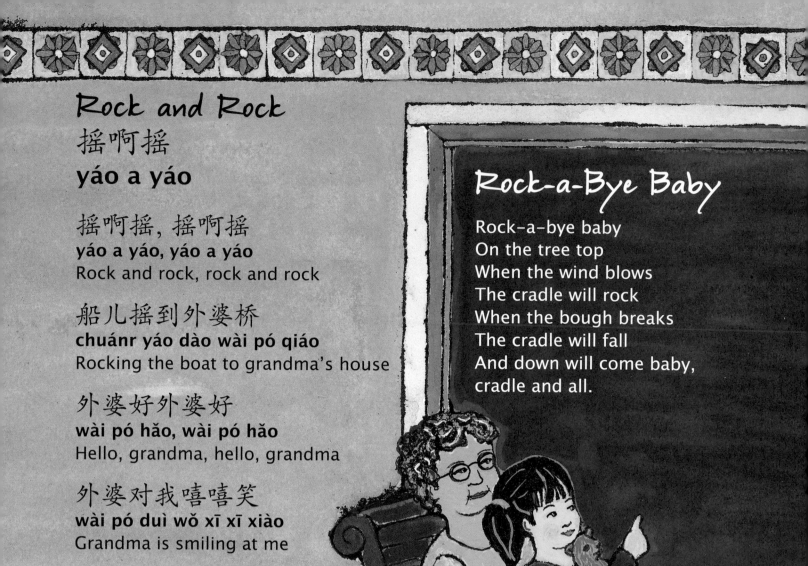

# Rock and Rock
## 摇啊摇
### yáo a yáo

摇啊摇, 摇啊摇
**yáo a yáo, yáo a yáo**
Rock and rock, rock and rock

船儿摇到外婆桥
**chuánr yáo dào wài pó qiáo**
Rocking the boat to grandma's house

外婆好外婆好
**wài pó hǎo, wài pó hǎo**
Hello, grandma, hello, grandma

外婆对我嘻嘻笑
**wài pó duì wǒ xī xī xiào**
Grandma is smiling at me

摇啊摇, 摇啊摇
**yáo a yáo, yáo a yáo**
Rock and rock, rock and rock

船儿摇到外婆桥
**chuánr yáo dào wài pó qiáo**
Rocking the boat to grandma's house

外婆说好宝宝
**wài pó shuō hǎo bǎo bǎo**
Grandma says, good baby

外婆给我一块糕
**wài pó gěi wǒ yí kuài gāo**
Grandma gives me a treat.

# Rock-a-Bye Baby

Rock-a-bye baby
On the tree top
When the wind blows
The cradle will rock
When the bough breaks
The cradle will fall
And down will come baby,
cradle and all.

## Star Light, Star Bright

Star light, star bright
First star I see tonight
I wish I may
I wish I might
Have the wish I wish
tonight.

## My Mama's Eyes

妈妈的眼睛
**māma dē yǎn jīng**

美丽的美丽的天空里
**měi lì de  měi lì de tiān kōng lǐ**
Beautiful beautiful sky

出来了光亮的小星星
**chū lái liǎo guāng liàng de xiǎo xīng xīng**
Little bright stars appearing

好象是我妈妈慈爱的眼睛
**hǎo xiàng shì wǒ māma cí ài de yǎn jīng**
Like my mama's loving eyes

妈妈的眼睛我最喜爱
**māma de yǎn jīng wǒ zùi xǐ ài**
I love my mama's eyes

常常希望我做个好小孩
**cháng cháng xī wàng wǒ zuò gē hǎo xiǎo hái**
She wishes me to be good

妈妈的眼睛我最喜爱
**māma de yǎn jīng wǒ zùi xǐ ài**
I love my mama's eyes.

# About the Chinese Language

### Written Chinese

Each Chinese character is pronounced as a single syllable and has its own meaning. Chinese writing was invented about 5,000 years ago. The characters we use today originated as pictograms—that is, drawings that represented things in nature, such as animals, rivers and plants. These written words gradually changed in appearance through the millennia, resulting in today's characters.

There are two systems for writing Chinese characters today. The "traditional" form is more complex. The "simplified" form is more simple and streamlined, and was created by the Chinese government to make reading and writing easier. Many characters are identical in the two forms. This book's Chinese characters are shown in simplified form. To download the rhymes in traditional form characters, please visit www.tuttlepublishing.com.

### Spoken Chinese

There are many dialects spoken in China. After 1913, the Mandarin dialect was chosen as the official spoken language in China.

An internationally-recognized phonetic system called pinyin is a way to express the sounds of the Chinese language, and to write them using the characters that English-speakers are more familiar with.

Whether you read the Chinese character or the pinyin equivalent, the sounds of Chinese are somewhat different than those of the English language. Listen to the CD to begin to understand how the Chinese sounds work (and how pinyin expresses them).

Mandarin Chinese is a tonal language, so along with the sounds themselves, each Chinese character also carries a tone.

These are the tone marks used in pinyin. They indicate for you which tone to use when saying a syllable:

  ¯  1st tone: high and level
  ´  2nd tone: high and rising
  ˇ  3rd tone: dipping low, then rising again
  `  4th tone: sharply falling

# Sing Along!

## Outside

## Inside

## Party

## Play

## Night

### Bonus Rhymes!